BEARS!

PAUL STICKLAND

I lay in bed,
with all my toys,
and thought I heard a *furry* noise...

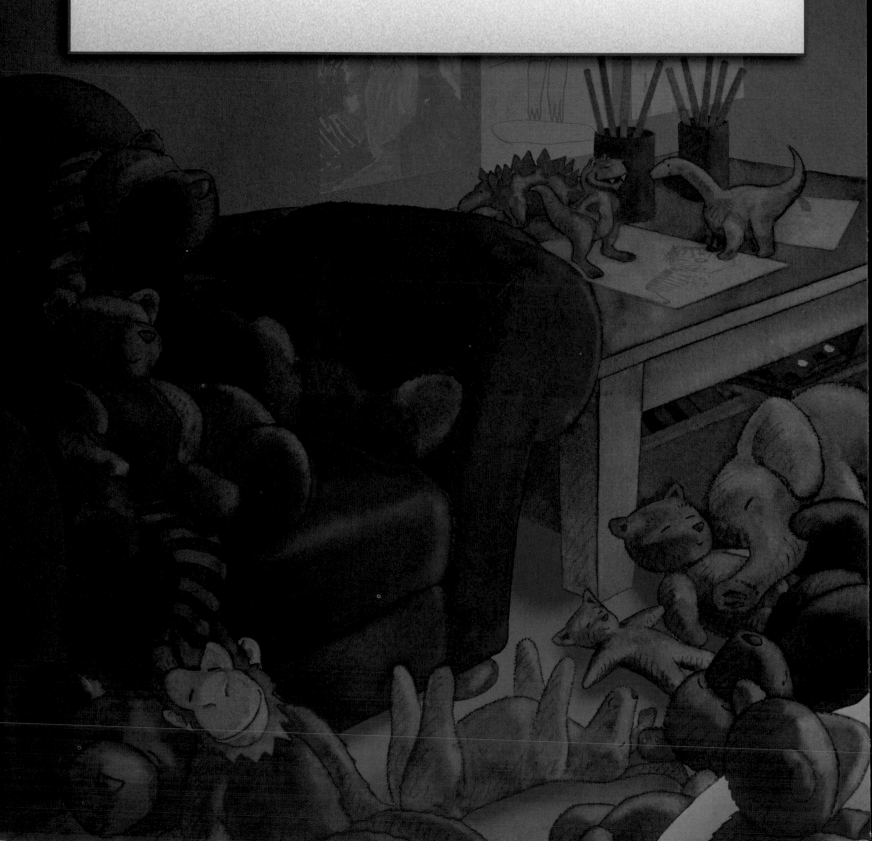

I peeped outside my bedroom door,
my eyes grew wide with what I saw...

For in the hall,
down by the stairs,
were lots of very friendly bears!

It seemed a party had begun
and everyone was having fun.
I wasn't scared, I couldn't be,
the bears were happy as can be!

It started out with just a few
and then their numbers grew and grew,
until you really couldn't hide
from bears who now were here, inside!

I thought I'd better tell my Mum
but soon the numbers had become
so great, I couldn't see the stairs,
for really far too many bears!

I thought I'd better tell my Dad
about the problem that we had.
I asked the bears to move aside,
ran to their room and went inside.

They seemed to be so fast asleep
but I had news I couldn't keep.
So up I jumped and gave a shake,
and *fairly* soon they were awake.

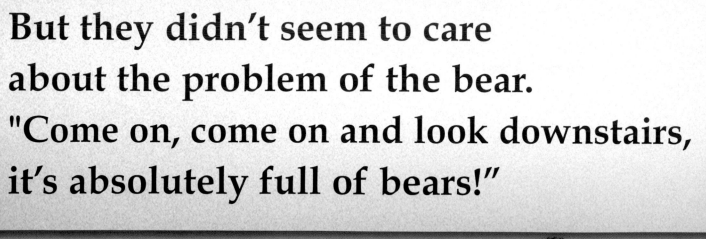

But they didn't seem to care
about the problem of the bear.
"Come on, come on and look downstairs,
it's absolutely full of bears!"

So Dad got up and shouted, "SHOO!"
and I went out and I looked too
but all those bears had simply gone,
except for just one special one.

So back in bed..
I tried to sleep...
but *then* I heard....
the sound of.....